DROUGHTS

MICHAEL WOODS AND MARY B. WOODS

LERNER PUBLICATIONS COMPANY
MINNEAPOLIS

To Matthew Woods

Editor's note: Determining the exact death toll following disasters is often difficult—if not impossible—especially in the case of disasters that took place long ago. The authors and the editors in this series have used their best judgment in determining which figures to include.

Lerner Publications Company
A division of Lerner Publishing Group
241 First Avenue North
Minneapolis, MN 55401 U.S.A.

Website address: www.lernerbooks.com

Library of Congress Cataloging-in-Publication Data

Woods, Michael, 1946–
    Droughts / Michael Woods and Mary B. Woods.
      p.   cm. — (Disasters up close)
    Includes bibliographical references and index.
    ISBN-13: 978-0-8225-6576-5 (lib. bdg. : alk. paper)
    ISBN-10: 0-8225-6576-5 (lib. bdg. : alk. paper)
     1. Droughts—Juvenile literature. I. Woods, Mary B. (Mary Boyle), 1946–
II. Title.
QC929.25.W66 2007
363.34'929—dc22   2006018980

Manufactured in the United States of America
1 2 3 4 5 6 – DP – 12 11 10 09 08 07

Contents

Introduction

PEOPLE IN NIGER NEED EVERY DROP OF RAIN THEY CAN GET. MUCH OF THIS WEST AFRICAN COUNTRY RECEIVES ONLY 4 INCHES (10 CENTIMETERS) OF RAIN EACH YEAR. THE WETTEST SPOTS GET LESS THAN 32 INCHES (81 CM). NIGER IS ALSO VERY HOT. BY COMPARISON, ARIZONA AND NEVADA, WHICH ARE MOSTLY DESERT, BOTH GET ABOUT 8 INCHES (20 CM) OF RAIN EACH YEAR. MOST OF THE 14 MILLION PEOPLE IN NIGER GROW THEIR OWN FOOD. WITHOUT RAIN, THEIR CROPS DON'T GROW AND THEY GO HUNGRY.

"Life is hard here," said Lawaly, a truck driver for the International Red Cross. "When it rains, the crops grow. When it doesn't—[it's the] Sahara." The Sahara is Africa's largest desert.

HUNGRY ANIMALS

A severe drought came to Niger in 2004. For several years, the weather had been drier than usual, but that year barely a trickle of rain fell.

Niger already is one of the poorest countries on Earth. The drought made Niger's people even poorer. It killed about 40 percent of the grass needed to feed their cattle and goats.

Cattle are very valuable. They provide milk and meat. People also sell them to get money so they can buy other things.

"The situation is terrible," said Abdoulye Adamou. "We have no food and our cattle are dying in front of our eyes because of a shortage of water and food."

Then the locusts arrived. These grasshoppers form swarms (large groups) when their food runs low—as it does in a drought. One swarm may have fifty million hungry bugs. Swarms land on farmers' fields and eat. What the drought didn't kill, the locusts ate.

These locusts swarmed during a drought in Mauritania, a country in West Africa.

"The locusts came at two o'clock," said Manomi Maïgomo, a farmer. "They ate and when they had finished at ten the next morning, they left." Maïgomo's crops were gone.

STARVING PEOPLE

By 2005 Niger was really in trouble. About 3.6 million of its poorest people—especially children—faced starvation. "Most of them are . . . hungry," said a doctor who was in Niger to help. "They're . . . skinny and starving without enough food." Many people were eating just one meal a day. Some ate grass and leaves to stop the hunger pains.

Natasha Quist described one boy she met in Niger: "He's one of six children. Three of his brothers and sisters already have died." People from around the world sent food and medicine to Niger. Relief workers went to Niger to help as many people as possible. But the drought went on and on, becoming a terrible disaster—an event that causes great destruction.

They're just sacks of skin and bones.

—Ofeibea Quist-Arcton, a reporter, describing children in Niger in 2005

The ongoing drought in Niger has caused food shortages.

What Are Droughts?

DROUGHTS ARE DRY TIMES WHEN PEOPLE DO NOT HAVE ENOUGH WATER. IN A DROUGHT, MONTHS OR YEARS MAY PASS WITH LITTLE RAIN OR SNOW. PLANTS DIE. GREEN FIELDS ON FARMS AND LAWNS IN CITIES TURN BROWN. RIVERS, STREAMS, LAKES, PONDS, AND WELLS DRY UP. WATER IN RESERVOIRS (LAKES WITH WATER FOR PEOPLE TO DRINK) GETS LOW.

A long drought can be a terrible disaster because water is so important. "Water is life," said scientist John Dohrenwend. "If you don't have it, the land can't support life."

The average person in the United States uses about 100 gallons (379 liters) of water every day. That's enough water to fill two bathtubs. A person in Cuba, an island country south of Florida, uses about 50 gallons (189 l) a day. "What's worse?" asked Roberto Cables, a resident who lived through a 2004 drought in Cuba. "Having no lights or having no water? You can always light a candle. But how do you replace water? With what?"

In the United States, the average person uses enough water every day to fill two bathtubs.

FARMS AND FACTORIES

Farmers need water to grow crops, such as wheat, corn, and soybeans. They also need it to raise animals. According to the U.S. Environmental Protection Agency, a cow drinks about 4 gallons (15 l) of water to make 1 gallon (4 l) of milk.

"If the rain doesn't come, the grass doesn't grow, and if the grass doesn't grow, **there is no way to feed the cattle."**
—Pam Houston, describing drought conditions in Colorado in 2006

Drought often causes farmers to lose their crops.

Water is important for turning some crops into other food products. It takes about 150 gallons (568 l) of water to make one loaf of bread, including the water needed to grow the wheat and to process it into flour. Growing and processing potatoes for one serving of french fries takes about 6 gallons (23 l).

Factories also need water to make products that people use in everyday life. It takes 24 gallons (91 l) of water to make 1 pound (0.5 kilograms) of plastic. Would you believe that making one new car uses 39,000 gallons (148,000 l) of water?

A DIFFERENT KIND OF DISASTER

Tornados, earthquakes, and fires have a sudden beginning and end. Everyone can see the damage right away. Droughts cause more damage than many other disasters. But the damage happens slowly.

WATER BY THE GALLON

The average person uses about 1 gallon (4 l) of water every day for drinking and cooking. Each toilet flush takes 5 to 7 gallons (19 to 27 l) of water. Five minutes in the shower uses 25 to 50 gallons (94 to 189 l). Washing your hands and brushing your teeth uses 10 to 20 gallons (38 to 76 l) in a day.

A drought can cause ears of corn to dry out before they are ready for harvest.

For the first few months, people may not know that a drought is happening. "It creeps up on you," said Don Wilhite, a scientist who studies drought. "And so it's often times hard to know when a drought begins."

Shelley Powers lived during a drought in Missouri in 2005. "We focus on weather that is destructive, such as with hurricanes and floods, yet hardly any notice is paid to drought," she said.

In 2002 severe drought caused High Rock Lake in North Carolina to shrink back from the shore.

ONE DISASTER LEADS TO ANOTHER

Droughts kill more people than many other natural disasters. That's because droughts in poor countries can cause famines. Famines are terrible shortages of food in which people die from hunger. As many as thirteen million people starved to death during one drought in China. People who don't get enough food or the right food also catch diseases easily. Drought victims may become sick or die from infections and disease.

In addition, droughts can lead to other disasters. Fires start easily in dry weather. Wildfires that destroy forests and homes are common during droughts. Long droughts may cause good farmland to become unusable. Fish and wild animals also suffer and die in droughts.

THE LOST COLONY

Drought may explain the mystery of Roanoke Island in North Carolina. In 1587 Sir Walter Raleigh established an English colony (settlement) there with 120 people. When an English ship returned in 1590, everyone was gone. The island had suffered a terrible drought. It may have forced the colonists to leave and live with Native American people nearby.

Drought led to dying fish in 2004 at the Lake of the Ducks in Rio Grande do Sul, Brazil.

1876–1878
CHINA

Drought in China in the late 1800s led to food shortages. Many adults and children died from hunger.

Rain is very important when people raise all their own food. Without enough rain, there is not enough to eat. Life was like that in China in the 1800s. The people relied on heavy rains falling at the right times. These rains kept farmers' fields green with rice, fruits, and vegetables.

Then for three long years, not a drop of rain fell on four provinces (states) in northern and central China. Millions of people lived in that area. At first people lived on food stored from before the drought and hoped for rain.

Soon, however, the food ran out. Residents began to starve. **"The people's faces are black with hunger,"** wrote Frederick Balfour, who was living in eastern China. People in nearby provinces couldn't send in any food to help. Those areas were suffering from another disaster—floods. Rivers overflowed and water flooded their farms and destroyed their crops.

It's hard to even imagine being truly hungry for one day. In China, people went without food for week after week. They had no hope of getting help. People are desperate when they are starving. They may do things they would never do otherwise. Starving people in China ate horses, dogs, cats, and rats. When all the animals were gone, they ate dirt and bark from trees to make their stomachs feel full. A few resorted to cannibalism (eating other people).

Many parents could not feed their children. Some sold their children as slaves. Others murdered their children. Balfour wrote, **"Parents have been known to kill [their children rather] than witness their prolonged sufferings, in many instances throwing themselves afterwards down wells."**

Wolves, foxes, and wild dogs also were starving because the animals they ate were gone. When it got dark, they attacked and ate people.

"Night traveling was out of the question," one disaster relief worker wrote. **"The wolves, dogs, and foxes soon put an end to the sufferings of any wretch who lay down to recover from or die of his sickness."**

It was one of the worst recorded famines in the history of the world. Between 9.5 million and 13 million people died because of the drought. Another 70 million suffered terribly but lived.

"They are dying by thousands upon thousands."

—Frederick Balfour, who witnessed the 1876–1878 drought in China

What Causes Droughts?

MOST DROUGHTS HAPPEN WHEN THERE IS A LONG PERIOD WITH BELOW-NORMAL RAIN OR SNOW. DROUGHT IS A NORMAL PART OF EARTH'S CLIMATE. CLIMATE IS NOT THE SAME AS WEATHER. WEATHER IS THE TEMPERATURE, CLOUDINESS, AND RAINFALL THAT HAPPEN FOR A FEW DAYS AT A TIME. CLIMATE IS THE WEATHER THAT HAPPENS OVER A LONG PERIOD OF TIME.

Droughts have always made life hard for people. A terrible drought in 3500 B.C. caused the world's first recorded famine. It happened in Egypt, when the Nile River (the main water supply) ran low for seven years.

JET STREAMS

The weather that brings drought moves over Earth in systems. The systems are masses of air in which the temperature, moisture, and other conditions are the same. Winds move these weather masses from one place to another.

In the United States and other areas, winds called jet streams move and steer weather masses. Jet streams are strong wind currents that blow about 20,000 feet (6,096 meters) above Earth's surface.

Most jet streams are thousands of miles long and hundreds of miles wide. These rivers of air are several miles deep. They can howl at more than 100 miles (161 kilometers) per hour.

FAMINE IN AFRICA

One of the worst droughts of the 1900s happened in the 1980s in the African country of Ethiopia. At least 400,000 people died in 1984 alone. They starved to death because not enough rain fell to grow food. By 1989, 1 million people had died. Hundreds of thousands of others left Ethiopia to live in other countries.

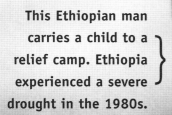

This Ethiopian man carries a child to a relief camp. Ethiopia experienced a severe drought in the 1980s.

" *[In 1985] the drought prevented the cultivation of crops and caused food shortages. People were also **too poor to afford to buy** food. They were also physically **too weak to work** and earn an income.* "

—Haji Zekiy, a religious leader and judge, describing a drought in the East African nation of Ethiopia

A jet stream has ridges and troughs that determine whether a drought will happen. A ridge is an area of high atmospheric pressure where the air sinks toward Earth's surface. Clouds and rain usually do not form in sinking air. That's why high-pressure weather systems usually mean nice, sunny weather.

A trough is an area of low atmospheric pressure where the air rises. Clouds and rain often form in rising air. Low-pressure systems usually mean cloudy, wet weather.

If an area has a jet stream with ridges that stay in place for a long time, a drought will occur. That's because the ridges will bring sunny, dry weather. They also will block air masses that could bring rain.

EL NIÑO AND LA NIÑA DROUGHTS

Meteorologists (scientists who study the weather) do not know exactly why jet streams change in ways that cause droughts. They do know that ocean temperatures and currents affect Earth's weather and climate. Temperature changes in the Pacific Ocean off the western coast of South America may lead to droughts.

Sometimes a wide band of water in the Pacific Ocean gets unusually warm for a few years. That warming is an El Niño. At other times, the water gets unusually cool, forming a La Niña. These changes in ocean temperature determine where storms form. In doing so, they lead to changes in rainfall. The changes can affect rainfall and other weather across the globe.

FAST FACT

The current of warm water known as El Niño usually appears around Christmas. This Christian religious holiday celebrates the birth of Jesus Christ, as described in the Bible. For this reason, fishers in Peru named the current El Niño. In Spanish, *el niño* refers to baby Jesus.

THE JET STREAM

The flow of the jet stream (strong wind currents that flow across the United States) affects where droughts occur. A ridge is an area of high pressure. High pressure means dry, sunny weather. A trough is an area of low pressure. Troughs mean cloudy, wet weather. Drought is likely when a ridge stays over the same area for a long time.

CANADA

HIGH PRESSURE

RIDGE

JET STREAM

TROUGH
LOW PRESSURE

UNITED STATES

MEXICO

During an El Niño, the Pacific Northwest states often are drier than usual. Parts of Central America and northern South America may also experience drier weather. During a La Niña, the midwestern United States may be drier than normal. El Niño and La Niña can also make weather in other parts of the world wetter.

An El Niño is especially bad news for people in Australia. Many El Niños have happened at the same time as bad droughts. People even call the great Australian drought of 1991 to 1995 the Long El Niño Drought.

PEOPLE LEND A HAND

Human activities can lead to droughts too. Cutting down a large number of trees and bushes leaves the ground bare. Too many cattle or other animals can kill grass and also leave bare ground.

Bare ground reflects more sunlight back into the air than ground covered with plants. The extra reflected sunlight may make the surrounding area hotter and drier. When rain does fall, it evaporates quickly, like water drying on a hot sidewalk. During evaporation, water changes from a liquid to a gas in the air. This rapid loss of water after a rainfall makes the ground even drier.

Once a drought is under way, the dry weather can cause plants to die. Having fewer plants means even more bare ground. The bare ground, in turn, means the drought will continue. As more land dries out, drought can spread.

SNUSTERS

A major drought in the midwestern United States took place in the 1930s. As the drought came to an end, blizzards (snow blown by strong wind) returned. The storms' strong wind also swept up dust, which mixed with the snow. People called these mixtures of <u>snow</u> and <u>dust</u> snusters.

In the summer, a grassy area can be up to 10°F (6°C) cooler than bare ground is. Heat reflecting off bare ground can make a bad drought worse.

1930S
THE DUST BOWL

Huge dust storms took place regularly in the midwestern United States during the 1930s.

Harley Holladay was playing outside one bright sunny day in 1935 near Dodge City, Kansas. In the distance, the thirteen-year-old saw what seemed like a huge, dark thunder cloud. But it was too big for a cloud. And it moved toward him too fast.

"I sprinted to the house to tell my parents that the dust was coming," said Holladay. *"The cloud caught me outside. . . . It was black as night. I got down on my hands and knees and tried to crawl toward the house. I finally felt the porch, and reached up and opened the screen door and crawled inside."*

For almost ten years, people all over the central United States lived with a great drought. It started in 1931 and affected about 60 percent of the country. Texas, Oklahoma, Kansas, Colorado, and New Mexico were so dry that people called this area the Dust Bowl. The Dust Bowl covered 97 million acres (39 million hectares) of land. A football field is about 1 acre (0.4 hectare), not counting the end zones.

largest migration in U.S. history. By 1940, 2.5 million people had moved out of the Dust Bowl. About 200,000 people went to California.

The migrants were poor. They tied furniture and other belongings on top

"The wind was blowing, it was dry, the cotton wouldn't come up, everything went wrong."

—Paul Westmoreland, of Oklahoma, on the 1930s Dust Bowl drought

This family is leaving Oklahoma. The drought of the 1930s caused many people to leave the area.

Most people in the Dust Bowl made their living as farmers. When their farms dried up, these people had no money. *"The land just blew away,"* a Kansas man said in 1936. *"We had to go somewhere."*

The drought brought about the

of cars. Then everyone crowded in. *"There was eight of us . . . in one automobile,"* said Roy Philips. *"We were really loaded down."*

The drought happened during the Great Depression (1929–1942). Many people in the United States lost their jobs. Even when people left the Dust Bowl, they had a hard time finding good-paying jobs.

The U.S. government tried to help the disaster victims. It gave jobs and money to people hurt by the drought and to other poor people. The relief program became a model for other government relief programs in future disasters. And the drought finally came to an end in the early 1940s.

Drought Country

ABOUT ONE BILLION PEOPLE LIVE IN AREAS OF THE WORLD WHERE DROUGHTS HAPPEN. DROUGHTS CAN OCCUR ALMOST ANYWHERE—IN WET OR DRY AREAS. ONE DROUGHT IN 2005 HAPPENED IN THE AMAZON RAIN FOREST IN SOUTH AMERICA. ANOTHER HIT AUSTRALIA, A VERY DRY COUNTRY.

Droughts become disasters when they affect people. A wild area where no people live could have no rain for years, but it might not be a disaster.

DROUGHTS IN THE UNITED STATES

Some areas of the United States are more likely to have droughts than other areas. People in parts of the central and eastern states notice droughts after only a few weeks of below-normal rain. In this area, people use water mainly from surface sources such as rivers and lakes. Even a

The Amazon River in South America had very low water levels during a 2005 drought.

LONG-DISTANCE EFFECTS

People far away from dry weather may suffer from a drought. This happens when a drought strikes areas that grow food that will be sold elsewhere. Some areas grow food to export (send to other countries). "People will starve in Africa because we had a drought," said Shelley Powers. She lived in Missouri, which exports corn and other grain.

few weeks without rain can make water supplies run low.

In arid (dry) regions in the western United States, people rely on wells and water in reservoirs. Here people can breeze through short periods with little rain. That's because plenty of water remains in wells and reservoirs during dry spells that last only a few weeks. But they notice longer dry spells.

States in the middle of the country often have the worst droughts. These states are Montana, North Dakota, South Dakota, Nebraska, Wyoming, Colorado, Kansas, New Mexico, Oklahoma, and Texas. People in this region rely on water from both the surface (rivers, lakes, and reservoirs) and wells. Farming is very important in many of these states. Farming requires a lot of water. Droughts can quickly affect both surface supplies and wells.

JAMESTOWN, VIRGINIA

A drought in Virginia almost kept Jamestown from becoming the first permanent English settlement in the United States. The settlers (colonists) landed in 1607, at the start of a long drought. Life was so difficult that they almost went back home. By the winter of 1609, food was so scarce that people dug up graves and ate corpses (dead bodies). One colonist killed and cooked his wife.

DROUGHTS AROUND THE WORLD

Some of the world's worst droughts have happened in the Sahel region of Africa. This broad strip of semi-desert is on the southern edge of the Sahara.

The risk of drought is also increasing in other areas near the edges of deserts. Unwise ways of farming and raising cattle in these areas may dry out the land. It can become desert. This spread of deserts is called desertification.

Serious droughts also happen again and again in other areas. Among these areas are China, India, Australia, Brazil, Chile, Bolivia, Ethiopia, and the Philippines.

DISASTER ZONES

Droughts can happen almost anywhere in the world. This map shows where some severe droughts have taken place in the last one thousand years. The boxed information describes major droughts discussed in this book.

EUROPE 2003

SOVIET UNION
1921–1923

CHINA
1876–1878 (83 million
people affected)

ASIA

EUROPE

EGYPT
1064–1072

AFRICA

INDIA 1900

SAHEL
1968–1988 (150
million people affected)

NIGER
2004–2005 (3.6 million
people affected)

AUSTRALIA
2002–2003 (19 million
people affected)

AUSTRALIA

NORTH AMERICA

UNITED STATES
early 2000s (50 million
people affected)

VIRGINIA
1609–1612

DUST BOWL
1931–1941 (5 million
people affected)

AMAZON RAIN FOREST
2005

SOUTH AMERICA

1968–1988
THE AFRICAN SAHEL

French planes dropped sacks of food in 1973 during a drought in the Sahel. The sacks broke open, and people had to collect the food bit by bit.

In some African countries, ants collect millet (a grain) that farmers drop while harvesting their fields. Ants store this rice-sized grain in their anthills to eat later on.

In 1984 Ahmedu Ali Ba watched people take the millet back. People in the country of Mauritania dug into anthills. As the angry ants swarmed out, people collected the kernels of grain one by one. The people were starving. Each bit of grain was precious food.

One of the worst droughts in history forced millions of people in Africa to search for food. The drought began in the late 1960s in the Sahel. This semi-desert region is on the southern edge of the Sahara. It stretches from Senegal on the Atlantic Ocean for 5,000 miles (8,000 km) across Africa. People suffered all across the Sahel—from Senegal through Mauritania, Mali, Burkina Faso, Niger, Nigeria, and Sudan to Ethiopia.

Parts of the Sahel get only 1 to 4 inches (3 to 10 cm) of rain in a normal year. The disaster began when even less rain fell in the late 1960s. Millet and other food crops didn't grow or produced little grain.

The drought also hurt nomads. These people raise cattle, which eat grass. When the grass in one area is gone, the nomads pack up and move their herds to another spot.

Cattle are the most precious thing the nomads own. Cattle give the nomads meat, milk, and hides (skins). Cattle also can be sold for money. When drought killed the grass, hundreds of thousands of cattle died. The nomads lost everything.

"We have no food, almost no camels, no seeds and no strength to move even if we knew where we could find those things so our children could live," said Youssouf. Before the drought, he

> ## "I am as helpless and dependent as a newborn baby."
>
> *—Youssouf, a nomad chief in the West African country of Mali, commenting on the region's drought in 1985*

was a powerful nomad chief in Mali.

By the 1980s, the drought had spread to neighboring nations. **"Drought has swept through the savannas [grasslands], deserts and coastlines of all parts of Africa,"** the United Nations reported. **"At least 150 million persons are faced with starvation in the twenty-four most seriously affected countries."**

The drought may have killed 1 million people. It affected 50 million other people, making them sick or poor, or forcing them to move away.

"Even the vultures [birds that eat dead animals] have fled," said Ahmedu Ali Ba. He said he hoped the drought would end soon. **"If not [for the hope,] I would just lie down and die."**

{ Both people and cattle are at risk when drought leads to food shortages. }

27

Measuring Droughts

MEASURING DROUGHTS IS IMPORTANT. PEOPLE NEED TO KNOW WHEN A DROUGHT HAS STARTED. THEY MUST KNOW HOW MUCH DAMAGE IT HAS CAUSED AND WHEN IT MIGHT END. THAT INFORMATION CAN HELP PEOPLE LIVE THROUGH A DROUGHT AND RECOVER FROM IT.

If government officials know a drought has started, for instance, they can ask people to conserve (not waste) water. People may have to take fewer baths and showers and not use water for lawns or washing cars. Conservation can stretch out the water supply and make it last longer.

During U.S. droughts, water bans are common.

Knowing about a drought's damage can help relief workers decide how much help to send. People need the most help in a long, bad drought.

Everyone in a drought wants to know when the dry spell has ended. That usually means that life can start getting back to normal.

DIFFERENT DROUGHTS

Measuring droughts is more difficult than measuring some other kinds of disasters. One reason is that droughts usually have no sudden start or end. Different groups of people also want to know measurements of different drought effects. The effects appear at different times.

Most people, for instance, are curious about whether we're getting less rainfall than normal. If so, a meteorological drought may have started. Farmers, however, want to know if an agricultural drought has begun. These droughts happen after meteorological droughts.

Rivers and reservoirs, such as this one, dried up during the 1995 drought in southern France.

"Here in my village in France, the river going by our house has completely dried up, except a tiny meter-long [yard-long] stretch of water which holds the few surviving fish."

—Gerome, describing a 2005 drought in France

In an agricultural drought, not enough water is in the soil for a particular crop at a particular time.

Officials who decide whether to ration (ask people to use less) water want measurements of how much water is in lakes, rivers, and under the ground. They are interested in hydrological drought.

TOOLS OF THE TRADE

To track a drought, scientists need to know how much rain has fallen. For this task, they rely on rain gauges. You may have a rain gauge in your backyard. A basic rain gauge is a cylinder that's open at the top with measurements marked on the side. The measurements may be in inches or centimeters.

Did you know that wind affects the accuracy of rain gauges? If a strong wind blows while it is raining, a lot of rain may hit the side of a rain gauge instead of falling inside.

Meteorologists (scientists who study weather) and hydrologists (scientists who study water) use special rain gauges. Their rain gauges have large funnels at the top. The funnels help more water fall into the gauges. The gauges measure rainfall in millimeters.

Scientists also use other types of rain gauges. The weighing precipitation gauge measures the weight of the rain that falls. One benefit is that it can also accurately measure hail, snow, and other forms of precipitation. The tipping bucket rain gauge shows how long it takes for 0.008 inches (0.2 mm) of rain to accumulate. This tells scientists how intense the rainfall was.

THE TREES TALK

Scientists read tree rings to tell when droughts happened. Trees grow wider by adding a new layer of wood each year. In a cut branch, the layers look like rings. Each ring is one year of growth. Trees grow fat rings in wet years and skinny ones in droughts. Counting the rings and checking their size give a history of drought in an area.

This high-tech rain gauge measures rain, snow, and other precipitation by weight. A wind shield is around the outside to prevent wind from interfering with the measurements.

TV DROUGHT MEASUREMENTS

The simplest measurement of drought is the one in newspapers and on TV weather programs. It measures drought as a percent of normal rainfall. Meteorologists keep track of how much rain an area gets each year for many years. That's the normal rainfall.

By comparing rainfall this year to past years, they can say that rainfall for July is 40 percent or 80 percent below normal. That measurement may mean that a meteorological drought has begun.

MR. PALMER'S INDEX

Another way to measure drought is with a drought index (a number scale). A drought index combines many different pieces of information to get a better picture of drought. An index may include information about precipitation (rain, freezing rain, snow, hail, and sleet), moisture in the soil, or water flowing in rivers.

In the 1960s, a scientist named Wayne Palmer invented the most popular drought index. It's called the Palmer Drought Severity Index. The Palmer Index uses rainfall and temperature information to measure dryness in an area.

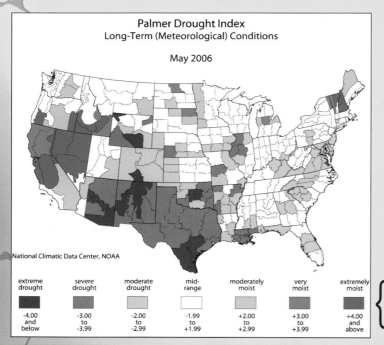

This map uses the Palmer Drought Severity Index to show where droughts occurred in the United States in May 2006.

PALMER DROUGHT SEVERITY INDEX

4.00 OR ABOVE	EXTREMELY WET
3.00 TO 3.99	VERY WET
2.00 TO 2.99	MODERATELY WET
1.00 TO 1.99	SLIGHTLY WET
0.50 TO 0.99	INCIPIENT WET SPELL
0.49 TO −0.49	NEAR NORMAL
−0.50 TO −0.99	INCIPIENT DRY SPELL
−1.00 TO −1.99	MILD DROUGHT
−2.00 TO −2.99	MODERATE DROUGHT
−3.00 TO −3.99	SEVERE DROUGHT
−4.00 OR BELOW	EXTREME DROUGHT

On the index, 0 is normal precipitation. Numbers below 0 mean a drought. A minus 2, for instance, is a moderate drought, while minus 3 is a severe drought, and minus 4 or below is an extreme drought. Numbers above 0 mean wetter-than-normal conditions. A 1 means slightly wet conditions, and 4 or above means extremely wet.

INDEX AFTER INDEX

Meteorologists also use several other indexes. These can give a better picture of drought conditions. One example is the Standardized Precipitation Index (SPI). It looks only at precipitation. It also uses zero to represent normal conditions. The SPI can spot the start of a drought months earlier than the Palmer Index.

The Crop Moisture Index, also invented by Wayne Palmer, measures growing conditions for farmers' crops. It uses the same number scale as the Palmer Index. Firefighters use numbers on the Keetch-Byrum Drought Index to spot dry conditions that can lead to forest fires.

Weather forecasters in the western United States may use several other indexes. In these states, snowfall is very important in the water supply. When snow melts in the spring, it helps fill rivers, wells, and reservoirs. The western United States also has mountainous land that is different from the terrain in the rest of the country. Yardsticks such as the Surface Water Supply Index help forecasters get a better measurement of droughts.

WORST OF THE WORST

The worst known drought in America started in 1579. It spread over the southwestern part of the country and lasted for at least twenty years. We know about it mainly because tree rings from that time were very thin.

African scientists work near a dust sensor in Niamey, Niger. They belong to the African Monsoon Multidisciplinary Analysis, a group that is trying to understand why the Sahel has had so many droughts.

2002–2003 AUSTRALIA

An Australian drought in 2002–2003 made life difficult for animals and humans.

Little Madeline White was three years old when her parents realized that she had never seen rain. The family lived on a farm in Queensland, a state in Australia. It was right in the middle of one of Australia's worst drought areas.

Rain is an unusual sight for most people in Australia. Next to Antarctica, it is the world's driest continent. And the weather has been getting drier. One terrible drought lasted from 1991 to 1995. In 2002 and early 2003, Australia had another drought. This one was the country's worst since record keeping began in 1910.

On February 23, 2003, Madeline saw rain for the first time. *"As soon as the rain started she came roaring into the room where we were reading,"* recalled Madeline's mom, Heidi White. *"She said 'Mummy, Mummy, it's raining, it's raining!' She dragged us outside and that was it. The clothes came off and she was in the mud."*

Madeline's dad quickly planted seeds in his fields. Other farmers did the same. But no more rain came. Their crops dried up and died. The drought continued.

Newspapers wrote stories about Madeline. She became famous around the country. People thought of her as a symbol for the terrible drought, the hopes of farmers, and their disappointment.

More than forty thousand farmworkers lost their jobs because of the drought. Farmers in some areas planted crops but had nothing to harvest because the crops all died. With nothing to harvest, the farmers couldn't make any money. *"Can you imagine [going] to work for three years without getting a [pay]check?"* asked Mal Peters, president of the New South Wales Farmers' Association.

With no food for their sheep and cows, farmers were forced to sell the animals. Many farmers sold some of their land. Others had to leave their farms and move to cities and look for new jobs. *"Everybody's in the same boat,"* said farmer Ian Burns. *"They're losing sheep [very quickly]. Tanks are drying up. There's no rain. You get a dust*

storm every second day." Madeline's dad, Paul White, had to take a job away from their farm. He bought a motorcycle to drive to the job. In 2004 the motorcycle skidded on a curve and crashed into a tree. Paul White died in the crash. *"If it wasn't for the drought, it wouldn't have happened,"* said Heidi White.

"It just goes on and on."
—Ian Burns, describing the 2002–2003 drought in Australia

In 2002 Australia's drought led to fires, such as this one in New South Wales.

Wildfires broke out all over the country. People living in big cities such as Sydney and Melbourne had to use less water. The drought cost the equivalent of U.S. $3.9 billion.

People Helping People

RELIEF AND RECOVERY WORK IN MOST DISASTERS STARTS AFTER THE
DAMAGE IS DONE. RELIEF REDUCES THE AMOUNT OF SUFFERING AMONG
PEOPLE INVOLVED IN A DISASTER. RECOVERY HELPS PEOPLE GET THEIR
LIVES BACK TO NORMAL. RELIEF WORK FOR DROUGHTS, HOWEVER,
USUALLY STARTS BEFORE THE DROUGHT IS DONE.

The amount of relief needed depends on how long the drought lasts. For a drought that lasts many years, the relief work may continue for many years. In contrast, people may not need much relief in a short drought. For short droughts, a few weeks of good rainfall can bring everything back to normal.

People suffer during a drought. But they don't all suffer in the same way. Drought victims need different things depending on where they live and how they earn a living.

FARMERS AND RANCHERS

Drought in the United States hurts farmers and ranchers more than any other people. Farmers earn a living by raising animals and growing and selling corn, wheat, and other crops. When drought makes crops fail, farmers can lose money. They may have to sell their land and move to another job.

Ranchers raise and sell cattle, sheep, and other animals. Those animals need water, grass, corn, and other food. When drought makes food scarce, ranchers may have to sell their animals and shut down their ranches.

Most drought relief in the United States goes to farmers and ranchers. They need money to keep farms and ranches running until a drought ends. During a drought in the early 2000s, for instance, the U.S. government provided farmers and ranchers with almost $3 billion in aid.

Drought caused this Texas cattle ranch to fail in 1953. The owner had to sell the ranch.

AROUND THE WORLD

Outside the United States, drought sometimes means hunger, sickness, and death for millions of ordinary people. That's especially true in poorer countries. Poor countries have little extra food to replace crops that don't grow during a drought. They also may not have money to buy food from nearby countries not affected by a drought.

These people need relief when a drought first begins. Yet it often takes time for the rest of the world to become aware of the need. People living in a drought-stricken area already may be starving by the time relief arrives.

Most adults can get along for months on little food. Babies and young children, however, may become sick and die without enough food or the right kind. Pregnant women must also have enough food for their babies to grow properly. People of all ages need plenty of clean water to drink every day.

FAST FOOD

The World Food Programme (WFP) brings most of the food to people in droughts. WFP is part of the United Nations, a group of more than 190 countries that work together to solve problems around the world. The United States and other countries give WFP food to pass out or money to buy the food.

Children at a feeding center near Nairobi, Kenya, eat high-energy biscuits.

In some years, WFP passes out more than 5 million tons (4.5 million metric tons) of food. The first food it supplies is often made for emergencies. WFP has special high-energy biscuits (crackers) that people can eat fast without any cooking. The biscuits contain more vitamins, minerals, and calories than ordinary crackers. Babies get their own special food.

40

This plane will deliver food to
southern Sudan, where a drought
led to famine in 1998.

WFP also makes sure to provide people with foods that are familiar to them. For example, in some parts of the world, people eat rice several times a day. They mix rice with beans or other vegetables to make a filling meal. If relief workers delivered potatoes instead of rice, people might have difficulty making meals.

HOME DELIVERY

Food usually comes to drought-stricken countries on big ships, each carrying more than 50,000 tons (45,000 metric tons). But getting food into a country is not enough. The food must be delivered to people who need it.

Delivery can be very difficult. Starving people often live far away from ports where ships arrive. Trucks may have to travel over rough roads. Sometimes there are no roads. Relief workers have to carry food on donkeys, camels, or elephants. In extreme cases, an airplane may drop boxes of food relief.

More than eleven hundred different relief organizations work with WFP to pass out food and help in many other ways. They include the International Red Cross and Red Crescent Movement, CARE, UNICEF, Doctors Without Borders, Save the Children, World Vision, and many others.

PEANUT BUTTER LIFESAVER

In the past, young children who were starving often had to be hospitalized and fed through a tube. Relief workers have found a better way to feed these children. It is Plumpy'nut, a thick peanut butter spread with added vitamins and minerals. Relief workers give packets of Plumpy'nut to mothers, who can give it to their children at home. It's fast, easy, and children love its taste.

Starving people sometimes leave their homes and gather in camps run by relief workers. The camps get regular deliveries of food and offer clean drinking water. They can provide special medical help to people who are sick.

Relief groups passed out bags of food in Niger in 2005.

AFTER THE DROUGHT

After a drought ends, people often need help getting their lives back to normal. They need money to buy seeds so they can plant crops again. People also have to replace cows and other farm animals that died or were sold during the drought.

"Before the drought I had 150 animals but now I have only ten left," said Kardar Vosh of Pakistan.

Recovery often means making changes in the way people live. These changes can help prevent future droughts or reduce the damage. Relief and recovery workers, for instance, may encourage farmers to plant crops that grow well even in very dry weather.

CAMELS NOT COWS

One change has happened in parts of Africa. Instead of just buying more cattle, relief workers have replaced those animals with camels. Camels are better able to survive very dry conditions. They also can plow farmers' fields and do other heavy work.

In some parts of the world, people do not have running water in their homes. Instead, they must carry their water from a well they share with other community members. In the past, women and girls often had to walk for hours every day to a well to get water. Then they carried it back home for drinking and cooking. Water is heavy. One gallon (4 l) weighs about 8 pounds (3.6 kg).

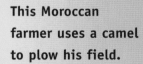

This Moroccan farmer uses a camel to plow his field.

Camels changed this situation. One camel can carry much more water than a person can. "[The camels] bring water enough for a number of households at a time," said Adde Lokko Aaro, in Ethiopia. "[Women] don't have to carry water on their backs."

Children walk across the bottom of a dried-up pond in eastern China.

> **In the past, there were only two ponds for the whole village where we could fetch water.**
>
> **If someone was hardworking, his family often had water to drink; if someone was lazy, he could only drink muddy water.**
>
> —Yeai, a farmer and weaver in southwestern China in 1997, talking about the work of hauling water by hand

The Early 2000s
UNITED STATES

In years with normal rainfall, Lake Powell, in Arizona and Utah, is high enough to cover all the light-colored rock surrounding the lake.

Almost half the United States was in a drought by the start of 2000. It stretched from the southeastern United States to the southern Plains. It continued along the Rocky Mountain states and into the Far West. In addition, an area of severe drought existed in the central plains.

"It's as bad as it was in the Dust Bowl," said Mike Johanns, who was governor of Nebraska. *"It looks like the moon. [Farmers] just don't spend money. Kids will go to school in the same clothes they wore last year."*

In the early 2000s, the drought was so bad that important sources of water started drying up. One was the Colorado River. It provided water and electricity to 24 million people in seven western states. By 2003 it carried less water than it had during the Dust Bowl years.

Lake Powell, in Utah and Arizona, stores water for many cities and farms in the West. Its water level dropped 30 feet (9 m) from 2002 to 2003. By 2006 the lake was 115 feet (35 m) lower than normal.

This was a modern U.S. drought. People did not run out of food and starve. Thousands of people did not pack up and move off their land, as they did during the Dust Bowl. Nevertheless, it was a disaster. Drought in wealthy countries usually is an economic (money) disaster. Farmers' crops die. Their families lose money because they have no crops to sell. Without food from local farmers, we must get food from other regions or other countries. That means everyone pays more at the grocery store.

In Missouri the drought dried up the wells from which Scott and Cindy Wood's family got their water. The family had to spend hours every week hauling water home in a tank on their old pickup truck.

"Inconvenience, time, gas, wear and tear on the pickup," said Cindy Wood. **"We go through it all just to get water."** The two Wood children, ages ten and seven, doubled up on

baths. When one finished, the other took a bath in the same water. The family also stopped flushing the toilet each time they used it.

The drought hurt the environment as well. Wildfires broke out in dry grass, bushes, and trees. Drought conditions lingered into 2006. By mid-year, 54,686 fires burned, compared to 39,240 in an average year. Most were in the Southwest and West.

Drought led to wildfires in California in 2003.

This cow got stuck in a muddy watering hole during a drought in Utah in 2002.

The Future

Disasters often teach us lessons. Those lessons can help people prepare for future disasters. The great Dust Bowl in the 1930s was one of the first teachers. That drought made the U.S. government act to prepare farmers for future droughts. One action was the establishment of the Soil Conservation Service (later renamed the Natural Resources Conservation Service).

Workers in this program taught farmers about better ways to plow the ground. Plowing cuts lines into the soil so a crop can be planted. Farmers usually plowed a hilly area in straight rows. But water ran off the soil easily instead of soaking in. In dry weather, wind blew down those rows and swept away the soil.

Contour plowing solves this problem. It cuts lines in curves that follow the shape (contour) of the land. More water soaks into the ground. More soil stays in place during droughts.

Drought returned to the Dust Bowl area in the 1950s. It affected a larger area than in the 1930s. But new plowing and other soil conservation actions worked. Farms suffered less damage than they had twenty years earlier.

BETTER WARNING SIGNALS

In the future, people may have more time to prepare for droughts because meteorologists will have better ways of predicting them. Good predictions will allow people to start using less water, build up supplies of food, and take other steps to survive a drought.

This Wisconsin farmer is using contour plowing. Plowing in curves means less water will run off the soil.

Meteorologists usually can't predict a drought more than a month in advance. To predict droughts, they use powerful computers and special computer programs, called models. In the future, meteorologists will have better models.

The models will include much more information about the rainfall, temperature, winds, and other things that cause drought. Computers of the future will be able to run those models faster. They may help predict not just whether a drought will begin but how long it will last.

LESS THIRSTY PLANTS

Farmers in the future will grow new kinds of corn, wheat, and other crops that need less water. In 2005 it took almost 4,000 gallons (15,000 l) of water to grow one bushel of corn. The plants that produce one bushel of wheat need 11,000 gallons (41,640 l) of water. (A bushel is about 60 pounds [27 kg] of corn or wheat.) Less thirsty plants would save water and grow better during droughts.

Scientists create plants that need less water by using genetic engineering. Genetic engineering changes the genes in living things. Genes

are tiny structures in the cells of all living things. They help determine traits, such as hair color for a person or height for a sunflower. Specific genes in corn and wheat determine how much water the plants need to live.

Researchers hope to create corn and other crops that need less water to grow.

> **"We have harvest if it rains,** otherwise not. . . .
> Nowadays the meteorological department gives
> advance information regarding rain and drought.
> **This helps us to prepare ourselves."**
> —Lakupati, an eighty-year-old female farmer in northern India in 1996

This meteorologist uses
sophisticated computer programs
to predict the weather.

CHANGING THE WEATHER

Have you ever heard this saying? "Everybody talks about the weather, but nobody does anything about it." In the future, it may be possible to change the weather to bring rain.

Weather modification means to modify, or change, naturally occurring weather in ways that help people. Scientists have been working on ways to make it rain since the 1940s. Cloud seeding involves releasing chemicals into the air from an airplane. The chemicals change any moisture in a cloud into drops of rain. New discoveries may allow scientists to squeeze rain out of air above areas suffering through a drought.

These planes are part of a cloud seeding project to bring more rain to Thailand.

BETTER IRRIGATION

Farmers in many countries use irrigation to grow food rather than depending on rainfall. *Irrigation* means "watering the land." Irrigation uses huge amounts of water. About 40 percent of the U.S. water supply goes to irrigate farm crops.

Nearby lakes and rivers supply some of the water for irrigation. But much of it comes from wells dug deep into the ground. Those wells use up underground water. It takes years for rain and snow to replace this groundwater. That makes it very important to avoid wasting irrigation water.

The most popular kind of irrigation involves letting water run through ditches scooped out between rows of crops. About half of that water, however, is wasted. It evaporates into the air and never gets into the roots of plants.

The irrigation system used to water these orange trees is called drip irrigation. The irrigation pipes have holes in them that release water only where it is needed. This system wastes less water than traditional irrigation systems.

In the future, more farmers will use new ways to irrigate fields. For example, the water will drip out of pipes laid on fields or under the ground. This method reduces the amount of water that evaporates.

A FUTURE WITH FEWER DROUGHTS

Droughts have been terrible disasters in the past. Millions of people have died in the famines that occurred in times of little or no rain. Droughts have driven people from their land and changed fertile land into desert.

Droughts will continue in the future. However, people will be better prepared for them. New advances in technology and better use of existing knowledge will reduce the damage from droughts.

XERISCAPE

People in dry areas often xeriscape the land around their homes and in parks. That word combines *xeri* (dry) and *landscape* (arranging plants on the land). Xeriscaping replaces lawns and some kinds of flowers with plants such as cactuses *(right)* that grow well in dry conditions. People don't have to water a xeriscape. It saves a lot of water.

DISASTER PREPAREDNESS

Preparation for a drought is very important. You and your family can do things before dry weather arrives that will make life easier during a drought. Knowing what to do during a drought also can keep a bad situation from getting worse. The things that each individual person does during a drought can make a big difference.

- Remember that water is precious. Always use it wisely. Then more water will be available when dry weather arrives.

- Talk with your parents about repairing dripping faucets and toilets that run. One drop per second wastes 2,700 gallons (10,200 l) of water per year.

- Follow the rules if your community rations water during droughts. Rationing rules say how much water you can use for watering the grass, washing cars, and other purposes.

- Remember that you can make a big difference. Just turning off the faucet while brushing your teeth, for instance, can save 10 to 20 gallons (38 to 76 l) of water every day.

- Many states and communities have drought preparedness plans. These plans give advice that fits the needs of your own area. Check for a copy of the plan on government websites or call government offices.

- During a drought, and in other times, too, never pour water down the drain when there may be another use for it. Use it to water indoor plants or the garden.

Timeline

3500 B.C. The first recorded famine takes place in Egypt when the Nile River runs low for seven years.

A.D. 1064–1072 The Nile River in Egypt is too low to allow the fields to be irrigated. In an eight-year-long famine, 40,000 people die.

1199 The Nile River is once again too low to provide irrigation for the crops. This time 100,000 Egyptians die from famine.

1587 Sir Walter Raleigh brings 120 people to establish a settlement in America.

1590 A passing ship discovers that Raleigh's settlement has disappeared, probably because of a severe drought.

1607–1612 A drought in Jamestown, Virginia, causes serious problems for the first English settlers in the United States *(above)*.

1769 When no rain falls for a year and a half in northern India, a three-year famine kills about 3 million people.

1833 Following a drought in Madras, India, 200,000 people die from starvation.

1871 The Peshtigo, Wisconsin, wildfire, the worst recorded forest fire in North America, occurs after a long period of drought.

1876–1878 Drought in northern and central China causes a famine that kills between 9.5 and 13 million people. This number includes the 3 million people who died of cholera from contaminated water.

1900 Between 1 million and 3.7 million people die from starvation and disease after a drought in India *(left)*.

1907 A drought in China causes major starvation and kills approximately 24 million people.

1921–1923 A severe drought in the Ukraine and the Volga regions of the Soviet Union *(below right)* causes an estimated death toll of 3 million people. It leaves one of the most productive regions of the Soviet Union a complete wasteland.

1928–1930 Northwestern China is the site of a drought where 3 million people die of famine.

1931–1941 The Dust Bowl, the longest drought of the 1900s in the United States, occurs. About 50 million acres (20 million hectares) of topsoil blows away. Thousands die and 2.5 million people leave the Great Plains in search of a better life.

1941–1943 Drought and famine in China kill 3 million people.

1965–1967 An estimated 1.5 million people die from starvation after a drought in India.

1968–1988 A drought in the African Sahel affects twenty-four countries. As many as 150 million people face starvation.

1991–1995 An El Niño drought in Australia lasts for four years.

2002–2003 Much of Australia experiences a drought *(left)*. The drought hits the state of Queensland especially hard.

2004–2005 Niger suffers from severe drought, followed by swarms of locusts.

2006 An estimated 60 percent of the United States faces drought conditions. Central and southern regions of the country experience the most severe drought.

Glossary

agricultural drought: when there is not enough water to raise crops and farm animals

conserve: to use water wisely and to use as little water as possible

desertification: the spread of deserts

drought: a time of dry weather with below-normal rainfall

dust storm: a windstorm that blows clouds of dust across an area

famine: a shortage of food that causes many people to die from hunger

genes: tiny structures inside cells that help determine the traits of plants and animals

genetic engineering: changing the genes in plants and animals to give them new traits

hydrological drought: a time when rivers and other water sources are low or dry up

meteorological drought: a time when precipitation is below normal

migration: movement from one region to another

Palmer Drought Severity Index: a scale that uses rainfall and temperature to measure the severity of a drought

precipitation: water that falls in the form of rain, freezing rain, snow, hail, or sleet

ration: to require people to use less water during a drought

weather modification: changing the weather to make rain or other conditions that people want

xeriscape: landscaping with plants that grow well in dry conditions. Xeriscaping conserves water.

Places to Visit

Cimarron National Grasslands in Elkhart, Kansas
http://www.fs.fed.us/r2/psicc/cim/
Take a self-guided tour through the rolling sagebrush prairie, and see the type of grassland that Kansas farmers plowed in the 1930s.

Kansas City Public Library in Kansas City, Kansas
http://www.kckpl.lib.ks.us/
You can see a collection of magazines and newspaper articles on droughts in Kansas.

Weedpatch Camp in Bakersfield, California
http://www.weedpatchcamp.com/
At Weedpatch Camp, the government provided a safe environment for migrants in the 1930s. Migrant workers still use the camp. The camp holds a Dust Bowl Festival once a year.

Wessels Living History Farm near York, Nebraska
http://www.livinghistoryfarm.org/
Wessels Living History Farm near York, Nebraska, has been reconstructed to show how agriculture has changed in the last one hundred years. Included on this 145-acre (59-hectare) farm is a house that is typical of an early twentieth-century farmhouse.

Yakima Valley Museum in Yakima, Washington
http://yakimavalleymuseum.org/
The museum has a 1930s pickup truck that was used by migrants going west during the Dust Bowl. The museum also has a large collection of farm tools.

Source Notes

4 Tom McRae, "This is Not Another Act of God— This Is Ingrained Poverty," *Observer* (London), August 7, 2005, http://observer.guardian.co.uk/ international/story/0,6906,1544099,00.html (October 28, 2005).

4 Idy Barou, "Bringing Relief to Niger's Hungry," *BBC News*, July 7, 2005, http://news.bbc.co .uk/go/pr/fr/-/1/hi/world/africa/4675379.stm (October 30, 2005).

5 Loetitia Raymond, "Today We Will Eat Our Fill, and I Will Have the Energy to Labour in the Fields," *Care.ca*, August 2005, http://Care.ca/work/ emergency/africa2005/nigerFarmer_e.shtm (November 5, 2005).

5 Jacki Lyden, "Profile: Food Shortages in Niger," *National Public Radio*, July 31, 2005, http://nl.newsbank .com/nl-search/we/Archives?p_action=doc&p_docid =10BB84D8C6F8 (October 28, 2005).

5 Neal Conan, "The Problems of Preventing Famine," *NPR.org*, July 26, 2005, http://www .npr.org/templates/story/story.php?storyId= 4771717 (August 9, 2006).

5 Ed Gordon and Ofeibea Quist-Arcton, "Niger Update: On the Verge of Famine Crisis," *NPR.org*, August 8, 2005, http://www.npr.org/templates/ story/story.php?storyId=4790174 (August 9, 2006).

6 Emily Sohn, "A Dire Shortage of Water," *Science News for Kids*, August 24, 2004, http://www .sciencenewsforkids.org/articles/20040825/ Feature1.asp (October 31, 2005).

6 Mary Murray, "Cuba Suffers Through Worst Drought in History," *msnbc.msn.com*, June 21, 2004, http://msnbc.msn.com/id/5262324 (October 7, 2005).

7 Pam Houston, "Parched on the Range," *New York Times*, June 11, 2006, 4.13.

10 Don Wilhite, interview by Scott Simon, *Weekend Edition Saturday*, NPR, September 21, 2002, http://www.npr.org/templates/story/story.php?storyId=1150387 (August 9, 2006).

10 Shelley Powers, e-mail message to authors, October 27, 2005.

13 Lee Davis, *Natural Disasters* (New York: Facts on File, 2002), 111.

13 Ibid., 110.

13 Ibid., 111.

13 Ibid., 110.

15 "Mountain Voices: Oral Testimonies from North Wollo, Ethiopia," *mountainvoices.org*, n.d., http://www.mountainvoices.org/e_th_migration.asp (August 9, 2006).

20 Phillip Hoose, *We Were There, Too! Young People in U.S. History* (New York: Farrar, Straus & Giroux, 2001), 196.

21 "Mass Exodus from the Plains," *PBS.org*, n.d., http://www.pbs.org/wgbh/amex/dustbowl/peopleevents/pandeAMEX08.html (November 11, 2005).

21 Interview with Roy Philips, "Interview about Life in Tennessee," *Voices from the Dust Bowl: The Charles L. Todd and Robert Sonkin Migrant Worker Collection, 1940–1941*, August 13, 1941, http://memory.loc.gov (October 29, 2005).

21 T. H. Watkins, *The Hungry Years: A Narrative History of the Great Depression in America* (New York: Henry Holt, 1999), 434.

22 Shelley Powers, e-mail message to authors, October 27, 2005.

27 Victoria Brittain, "In the Desert, the Suffering Is Spread Thin," *Guardian Newspapers Limited*, June 17, 1985, 6.

27 "Crisis in Africa," *UN Chronicle*, March 1984, 1.

27 Victoria Brittain, "In the Desert, the Suffering Is Spread Thin," *Guardian Newspapers Limited*, June 17, 1985, 6.

27 Richard Critchfield, "In Africa's Drought-Stricken Sahel, 'Even the Vultures Have Fled,'" *csmonitor.com*, April 9, 1984, http://www.csmonitor.com/1984/0409/040930.html (August 9, 2006).

29 "European Droughts: Your Experiences," *BBC News*, August 24, 2005, http://news.bbc.co.uk/2/hi/europe/4637697.stm (August 9, 2006).

36 David Murray, "Tragedy of Madeline, Face of the Drought," *Sunday Mail* (Queensland, AUS), October 9, 2005, 6.

37 Michael Byrnes, "Droughts Show Dark Side of Hot, Dry, Sunny Australia," *Washington Post*, June 5, 2005, A24.

37 Lockyer, "Farmers Face Worst Droughts in 100 Years."

37 Murray, "Tragedy of Madeline, Face of the Drought."

37 Paul Lockyer, "Farmers Face Worst Droughts in 100 Years," *abc.net.au*, June 11, 2002, http://www.abc.net.au/7.30/content/2002/s720415.htm (October 30, 2005).

44 Patrick Fuller, "Drought Relief Arrives for Nomads of Pakistan," *ifrc.com*, March 8, 2001, http://www.ifrc.org/docs/news/01/030802 (November 5, 2005).

44 "Drought Relief in Southern Ethiopia," *oxfamamerica.org*, May 13, 2002, http://www.oxfamamerica.org/whatwedo/where_we_work/ethiopia/news_publications/art2630.html (August 9, 2006).

45 "Mountain Voices: Oral Testimonies from Northeast and Southwest China," mountainvoices.org, n.d., http://www.mountainvoices.org/china.asp (August 9, 2006).

46 Martin Kasindorf, Patrick McMahon, Traci Watson, and Deborah Sharp, "Drought Likely to Spare U.S.

Economy as Whole," *USA Today*, October 6, 2005, http://www.usatoday.com/news/nation/2002-08-25-drought_x.htm (August 9, 2006).

47 Shashank Bengali, "In Northwest Missouri, Drought Alters Quality of Life," *Kansas City (MO) Star*, January 13, 2003, A1.

47 Ibid.

51 "Mountain Voices: Oral Testimonies from Garhwal and Kumaon, India," *mountainvoices.org*, n.d., http://www.mountainvoices.org/i_th_water.asp (August 9, 2006).

Selected Bibliography

Allaby, Michael. *Droughts*. New York: Facts on File, 2003.

Bonnifield, Mathew Paul. *The Dust Bowl: Men, Dirt and, Depression*. Albuquerque: University of New Mexico Press, 1979.

Burt, Christopher C. *Extreme Weather: A Guide & Record Book*. New York: W. W. Norton, 2004.

Collier, Michael, and Robert H. Webb. *Floods, Droughts, and Climate Change*. Tucson: University of Arizona Press, 2002.

Davis, Lee. *Natural Disasters*. New York: Facts on File, 2002.

Engelbert, Phillis. *Dangerous Planet: The Science of Natural Disasters*. Detroit: UXL, 2001.

Gregory, Kenneth John, ed. *The Earth's Natural Forces*. New York: Oxford University Press, 1990.

Restless Earth: Disasters of Nature. Washington, DC: National Geographic Society, 1997.

Spignesi, Stephen J. *The 100 Greatest Disasters of All Time*. New York: Citadel Press, 2002.

Vogel, Carole Garbury. *Nature's Fury: Eyewitness Reports of Natural Disaster*. New York: Scholastic Reference, 2000.

Watkins, T. H. *The Hungry Years: A Narrative History of the Great Depression in America*. New York: Henry Holt, 1999.

Zabrowski, Ernest, Jr. *Perils of a Restless Planet: Scientific Perspectives on Natural Disasters*. Cambridge, UK: Cambridge University Press, 1997.

Further Resources

BOOKS

Bender, Lionel. *Heat and Drought*. Austin, TX: Raintree Steck-Vaughn, 1998. This book explains the importance of water in developing countries.

Cooper, Michael L. *Dust to Eat: Drought and Depression in the 1930s*. New York: Clarion Books, 2004. This title explains the economic conditions of the United States during the 1930s. It tells how ordinary people struggled to survive during the Dust Bowl.

Hesse, Karen. *Out of the Dust*. New York: Scholastic Press, 1997. This novel won the Newbery award from the American Library Association in 1998. It chronicles the hardships and horrors of life on an Oklahoma wheat farm in the 1930s.

Jackson, Alison. *Rainmaker*. Honesdale, PA: Boyds Mill Press, 2005. In this novel, it is 1939 in Frostfire, Florida, and the town is desperate for rain. The townspeople hire a Mississippi rainmaker, Miss Lillie Stoate, in the hopes that she can bring enough rain to save their orange groves.

Levey, Richard H. *Dust Bowl! The 1930s Black Blizzards*. New York: Bearport Publishing, 2005. This book tells the story of the worst of the "black blizzards" that struck the Great Plains in 1935.

Meltzer, Milton. *Driven from the Land*. New York: Benchmark Books, 2000. Meltzer examines the political, economic, and social reforms that helped heal the wounds caused by the Dust Bowl and the Great Depression.

Peterson, Jeanne Whitehouse. *Don't Forget Winona*. New York: Joanna Cotler Books, 2004. This illustrated story, told in poetry format, tells of a farm family's travel west along Route 66 to escape the devastation of the Dust Bowl.

Stanley, Jerry. *Children of the Dust Bowl: The True Story of the School at Weedpatch Camp*. New York: Crown, 1992. This is a true story of a school that was started by Leo Hart and built by the residents of Weedpatch Camp in California. Students studied animal care and aircraft mechanics as well as traditional subjects.

Woods, Michael, and Mary B. *Fires*. Minneapolis: Lerner Publications Company, 2007. Learn more about fires, a common result of droughts.

WEBSITES AND FILMS

Biography of Hugh Hammond Bennett
http://www.nrcs.usda.gov/about/history/bennett.html
Read about Hugh Hammond Bennett, called the father of soil conservation, who urged the U.S. Congress to enact conservations laws.

Dust Storm Safety
http://www.nws.noaa.gov/om/brochures/duststrm.htm
These tips from the National Weather Service will keep you safe from the dangers of dust storms.

Kansas History Online
http://www.kansashistoryonline.com/ksh/ArticlePage.asp?artid=104
Read about the dust storms in Kansas, especially the huge one on April 14, 1935.

Voices from the Dust Bowl
http://memory.loc.gov/ammem/afctshtml/tshome.html
The Library of Congress in Washington, D.C., maintains this site as part of its American Memory project. The collection contains audio recordings, photographs, and written accounts of Dust Bowl migrants.

Xeriscape Colorado Website
http://www.xeriscape.org
The Colorado Water Wise Council sponsors this site. It gives information about using water efficiently.

Great Depression & the New Deal. VHS and DVD. Bala Cynwyd, PA: Schlessinger Video Production, 2003. This video shows, through film footage and interviews with survivors, the hard times in the United States during the 1930s.

Natural Disasters. VHS and DVD. New York: Dorling Kindersley, 1997.
This video gives background information on the forces that shape Earth.

Surviving the Dust Bowl. VHS. Alexandria, VA: PBS, 1998. This video has footage of the devastation of the Dust Bowl and many survivor stories and photographs.

Weather. DVD. London: BBC, 2003.
Donal McIntyre is the daredevil host of this documentary. It covers wind, water, heat, and cold extremes of weather.

Index

Photo Acknowledgments

The images in this book are used with the permission of: © Ami Vitale/Getty Images, p. 1; © Brown Brothers, pp. 3, 20; © Fred Hoogervorst/Panos Pictures, p. 4; © Daniel Berehulak/Getty Images, p. 5; © Dorling Kindersley/Getty Images, p. 6; © Inga Spence/Visuals Unlimited, p. 7; © Karlene Schwartz, pp. 8, 19; © David Sieren/Visuals Unlimited, p. 9; AP Images/The News & Observer, Chuck Liddy, p. 10; © Flavio Neves/epa/CORBIS, p. 11; Illustrated London News Picture Library, p. 12; © Keystone/Hulton Archive/Getty Images, p. 15; © Tim Boyle/Getty Images, pp. 17, 55; Library of Congress, p. 21 (LC-USF33-12312-MI); © Raimundo Valentim/epa/CORBIS, p. 22; © Alain Nogues/CORBIS SYGMA, p. 26; © Alain Nogues/Sygma/CORBIS, pp. 27 (both); AP Images/Charles Rex Arbogast, p. 28; © Pascal Parrot/Getty Images, p. 29; © Dr. James W. Richardson/Visuals Unlimited, p. 30; Photo by Molly Cavaleri/USDA Forest Service, p. 31; National Climatic Data Center, NOAA, p. 32; © age fotostock/SuperStock, p. 33; © Frederic Garlan/AFP/Getty Images, p. 35; © Reuters/CORBIS, pp. 36, 52; © Dean Sewell/Panos Pictures, p. 37; © A. Y. Owen/Time & Life Pictures/Getty Images, p. 39; AP Images/Khalil Senosi, p. 40; © Paul Lowe/Panos Pictures, p. 41; © John Schults/Reuters/CORBIS, p. 42; © Issouf Sanogo/AFP/Getty Images, p. 43; © Gerald & Buff Corsi/Visuals Unlimited, p. 44; © China Photos/Getty Images, p. 45; © Peter Essick/Aurora/Getty Images, p. 46; AP Images/Douglas C. Pizac, File, p. 47 (left); © NASA/CNP/CORBIS, p. 47 (right); © Richard Hamilton Smith/CORBIS, p. 49; PhotoDisc Royalty Free by Getty Images, p. 50; © Scientifica/Visuals Unlimited, p. 51; © Mark E. Gibson/Visuals Unlimited, p. 53; © Doug Sokell/Visuals Unlimited, p. 54; © North Wind Picture Archives, p. 56 (top); © Bettmann/CORBIS, p. 56 (bottom); © Albert Harlingue/Roger Viollet/Archive Photos/Getty Images, p. 57 (top); © David Gray/Reuters/CORBIS, p. 57 (bottom).

Front cover: © Mark Henley/Panos Pictures

About the Authors

Michael Woods is a science and medical journalist in Washington, D.C., who has won many national writing awards. Mary B. Woods is a school librarian. Their past books include Lerner Publications' eight-volume Ancient Technology series. The Woods have four children. When not writing, reading, or enjoying their grandchildren, the Woods travel to gather material for future books.